leapfrog

Mr Spotty's Potty

First published in 2000 by
Franklin Watts
96 Leonard Street
London
EC2A 4XD

Franklin Watts Australia
14 Mars Road
Lane Cove
NSW 2066

A CIP catalogue record for this book is available
from the British Library.

ISBN 0 7496 3711 0

Series Editor: Louise John
Series Advisor: Dr Barrie Wade
Series Designer: Jason Anscomb

Printed in Hong Kong

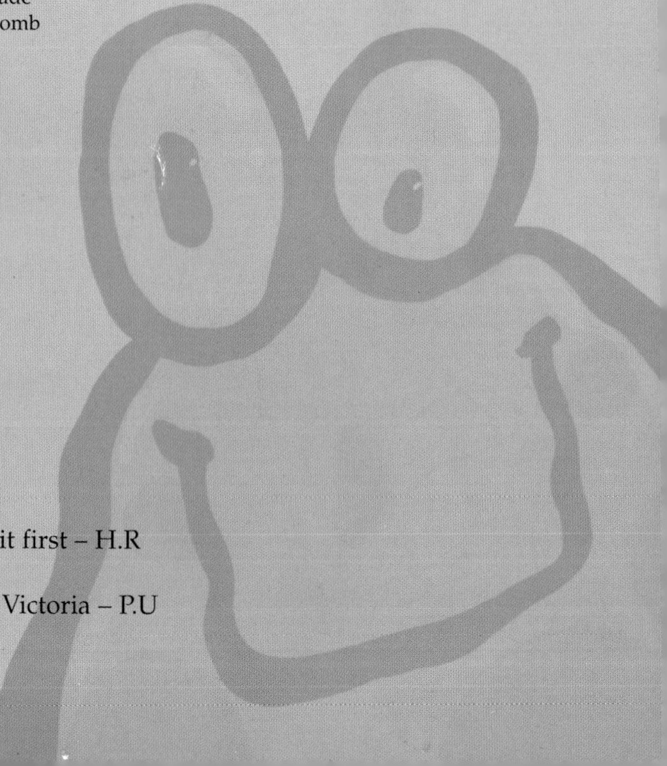

For Agnes, who heard it first – H.R

For Janet, Graeme and Victoria – P.U

Mr Spotty's Potty

by Hilary Robinson

Illustrated by Peter Utton

W

FRANKLIN WATTS

NEW YORK•LONDON•SYDNEY

Mr Spotty's potty
sits by his front door.

He puts lots of seeds
in it ...

... and waits for rain
to pour.

Dot, his dog, just nods at people who go by.

They stop and look
at all the flowers ...

... that grow up to the sky.

One day, Dot got fed up just sitting by the door.

She got up and went
inside ...

... and sat upon the floor.

That day, when big drops of rain fell down ...

... the flowers, they did not grow.

"Why?" said Mr Spotty.

"I really do not know!"

He took the potty
in the house and
put it down by Dot.

"They will not grow
in here," he said.

"The room is much too hot!"

But grow they did,
up and up ...

... and then they did
not stop.

They grew up two floors
of the house ...

... and up and out the top.

Then Mr Spotty knew,
as it was plain to see ...

29

That Dot would use
the potty ...

... to do a little wee!

Leapfrog has been specially designed to fit the requirements of the National Literacy Strategy. It offers real books for beginning readers by top authors and illustrators.

There are five other humorous stories to choose from:

The Bossy Cockerel ISBN 0 7946 3708 0

Written by **Margaret Nash**, illustrated by **Elisabeth Moseng**

A traditional farmyard story with a twist. Charlie the Cockerel is very bossy indeed. The hens think it's time he got his come-uppance ...

Bill's Baggy Trousers ISBN 0 7496 3709 9

Written by **Susan Gates**, illustrated by **Anni Axworthy**

A frivolous fantasy story about Bill and his new, baggy trousers, which turn out to be a lot more fun than he could have imagined!

The Cheeky Monkey ISBN 0 7496 3710 2

Written by **Anne Cassidy**, illustrated by **Lisa Smith**

A hilarious story about a little girl with a vivid imagination who encounters a monkey hiding in her treehouse. Read all about the exploits of Wendy as she tries to make the mischievous monkey leave.

Little Joe's Big Race ISBN 0 7496 3712 9

Written by **Andy Blackford**, illustrated by **Tim Archbold**

An outrageously silly story about the adventures of Little Joe as he runs an egg and spoon race that turns out to be more of an experience than he bargained for!

The Little Star ISBN 0 7496 3713 7

Written by **Deborah Nash**, illustrated by **Richard Morgan**

A fantasy story with an element of humour about a little star who no longer wants to live in the sky. His friend, the Moon, takes him on a magical journey to show him how much fun the sky can be.